The adventur

For Otto

David Milgrim

Ready-to-Read

Simon Spotlight

New York   London   Toronto   Sydney   New Delhi

For Carole and Zane
with hugs and pie

SIMON SPOTLIGHT
An imprint of Simon & Schuster Children's Publishing Division
1230 Avenue of the Americas, New York, New York 10020
This Simon Spotlight edition August 2020
SIMON SPOTLIGHT, READY-TO-READ, and colophon are registered
trademarks of Simon & Schuster, Inc.
For information about special discounts for bulk purchases,
please contact Simon & Schuster Special Sales at 1-866-506-1949 or
business@simonandschuster.com.
Manufactured in the United States of America 0720 LAK
2 4 6 8 10 9 7 5 3 1
Library of Congress Cataloging-in-Publication Data
Names: Milgrim, David, author illustrator.
Title: For Otto / David Milgrim.
Description: New York : Simon Spotlight, 2020. | Series: The adventures of Otto
Audience: Ages 3–5. | Audience: Grades K–1. | Summary: Otto goes from sad to
glad when his friend brings him a gift.
Identifiers: LCCN 2020021281 | ISBN 9781534465664 (paperback)
ISBN 9781534465671 (hardcover) | ISBN 9781534465688 (eBook)
Subjects: CYAC: Robots—Fiction. | Friendship—Fiction.
Classification: LCC PZ7.M5955 Fo 2020 | DDC [E]—dc23
LC record available at https://lccn.loc.gov/2020021281

See Otto feel sad.

No . . .
Wait . . .

Here comes Mo!

See Otto feel glad!

Oops!

Poor Otto.

No . . .
Wait . . .

Here comes Flop!

See Otto feel glad!

Oof!

Poor, poor Otto.

No . . .
Wait . . .

Here comes Pip!

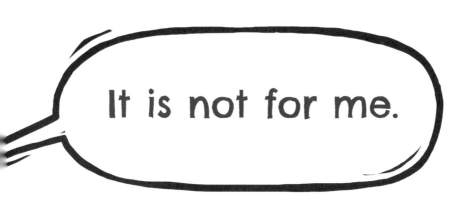

See Otto feel glad!